Love in the Wreckage

A Science Fiction Story Collection

Jesse Sprague

Copyright © 2021 Jesse Sprague

All rights reserved

The characters and events portrayed in this book are fictitious. Any similarity to real persons, living or dead, is coincidental and not intended by the author.

No part of this book may be reproduced, or stored in a retrieval system, or transmitted in any form or by any means, electronic, mechanical, photocopying, recording, or otherwise, without express written permission of the publisher.

Cover picture from: Pixabay
Printed in the United States of America

Contents

Title Page
Copyright
Blind Black | 1
Streamlined Living | 14
Suneater | 28
Wreckage | 42
Awake | 46
Join Jesse's Mailing List | 67
Books By This Author | 69
The Best Gift... | 71

Blind Black

Impenetrable darkness surrounded Carika. After weeks in its nearly ceaseless embrace, she was no more used to it than she had been on the first day. Those creatures had put her here, though she didn't know why. And she couldn't help but imagine their gray skin and featureless masks hiding in the sightless corridor in front of her. She couldn't help but imagine their scythe-like weapons swinging toward her. Carika fought to repress the panic flirting at the edge of her senses at the imagined aliens. There was only blackness.

She pressed onward, afraid to stop moving lest she lose Daryl to the dark. Of the original group she'd arrived with in this maze of corridors, Daryl was the only one left. He was all that kept her from being completely alone. As close as madness hovered in the blackness' velvet folds now, she knew insanity would descend in full-fanged fury without the ever-present sound of his footsteps.

Daryl was getting too far ahead.

He might slow for her, but that was only if he was in control of himself. Carika couldn't count on that.

One more step. Her foot hit the slick ground. She reached out and touched walls of smooth glass on either side. She'd been here long enough to know the same smooth hard material loomed maybe half a foot above her head, and behind her... behind her a wall of glass followed, forcing her forward. If she held her breath, she could hear the soft whisper of the wall's motion.

The aliens did not permit Daryl and her to stop moving. She

didn't know why.

But she had her imagination.

Carika shuddered and stumbled a few more steps before listening for Daryl. If she lost him, she'd never find him again. Though she'd never encountered a fork in the tunnel, she knew they existed and seemed to appear whenever a person was alone. There had been nine people to begin with. Ten, if you counted the man who died coughing blood on the first day after they arrived in the tunnels.

The wheezing, wet sound of his death sometimes reverberated as a ghost echo in her ears.

Life hadn't always been like this. She'd been a normal woman—at least, in her own estimation. After a few rough turns in her life, Carika had needed a break, and a tropical vacation had sounded just right. A way to escape the all-consuming grief.

If she'd known that this was what escape looked like, she would have stayed home.

But the brochures had been lovely—rustic wood cottages and miles of nothing in every direction. A place to be alone. A place to let go of the baby she'd lost and the man who'd been unable to understand how much the loss of an unborn being could hurt.

Carika couldn't imagine wanting to be alone anymore. The dark had robbed her of that, robbed her of almost everything. If only it could take away the images of what came just before she arrived in this dark hell. Take away her memories of the strange disease that killed a woman in the airport, and then two more in front of her eyes at the resort. Each bleeding from their eyes, ears and noses, and by the end, coughing blood.

This was supposed to be my best vacation ever.

The sole of her sneaker caught on the slick floor and flipped under her foot. It had come unglued at the toe ages ago. Carika's hand shot out to catch herself on the wall.

"Daryl!" she shouted automatically. But his footsteps didn't pause. He wouldn't, not with *them* in his head. And they must be, or he would have slowed by now, waited for her.

Carika quickened her steps, carefully placing her feet to avoid another trip.

She reached up to touch the metal plate on her skull. The rough torn flesh at the edges of the plate made contact with her fingers. The weight of her pocketknife hung heavy in the pocket of her sundress. That was the only reason she was free of their influence. She'd managed to deactivate the software, or whatever the hell they were using to control Daryl.

She'd panicked when she found the implant in her skull. Jabbing at her head with a knife probably hadn't been wise—only luck had allowed her to not injure herself too much and to disconnect whatever technology the strange gray skinned creature had used to control Daryl.

The same technology that the aliens had used to control the others, leading them off into the dark. Nothing but echoes in the darkness remained of the other vacationers. They'd disappeared two at a time... until it was Carika and Daryl's turn.

Then there had been the day she thought she'd lost him. It couldn't have been long after they separated from the others, and she'd known she couldn't survive completely alone with the sightless blackness. She'd called for Daryle for hours until she gave up and sat down to weep. Then he found her again.

She couldn't lose him, not to the dark, and not to the implant.

If only she knew how to repeat the deactivation procedure on Daryl's implant. But she didn't. She wasn't even sure why it had worked when she'd panicked and hacked at her own chip—she only knew it had worked because she never felt the monsters' influence. What if she tried to deactivate his and it killed him, or made him worse? She couldn't endure the black tunnel alone—not even with the occasional comfort of a room to rest in—some nights even with a light.

Nothing scared her more than being alone. Not even the disease that had killed those people back at the resort. That would still be better than being lost in here, forever running, alone in the dark.

And Carika's fear ruled her. Nothing to do but chase after Daryl and pray they didn't get separated. *But I will lose him one of these days.*

Carika blinked, and her feet sped over unseen ground.

Were *they* there, watching in the dark? She could picture *them* as they had been at the resort—masked and hulking. In the dark, her imagination transformed them, and they became more monstrous. Their grey skin sagged more and their masks fell away, revealing diseased greenish skin and black beady eyes as empty and demonic as an insect's.

Daryl's smell filled the air. She collided with his back—a contact he didn't appear to register. Carika clung to him, feeling his solid warmth and breathing in his scent—male and human.

"Smells like soup tonight," Daryl said. His voice was deep and warm but cracked and dry.

Carika rubbed at her own throat. Water, like food, came once a day.

"You go left? I'll check right?" Daryl asked. It was *his* voice not broken and robotic as he sounded became when the chip controlled him.

"Sounds good." Carika spread her arms out. No walls met her fingertips. If she'd had any doubt that this was the end of their "day," the arrival of the food proved her enforced trek was over for now. It also meant they'd arrived in a room rather than the uniformity of the tunnel, as they did each "night." She wandered until her hand met the wall and she followed it, dragging her feet carefully over the ground, because if she did find the food left out for them, she'd better not spill it.

Across the room, Daryl whistled a soft tuneless drone. Carika's lips formed a smile. Thank God for Daryl.

She sniffed the air. Along with the usual damp scent came a drifting hint of cinnamon and cloves. Carika followed her nose until her toe tapped into something hard. She reached down to touch the rim of a bowl, then beside it another bowl.

"Daryl, over here." Carika sat and gathered both bowls to her. Then partially to lead him to her and partially to hear his response, she spoke again. "Do you think they'll turn the light on tonight? It's been so long... it seems so much longer than before. Can you hear anything through the chip? Have they told you?"

"No. Sorry. It's quiet."

Carika sipped the soup. "Tastes good. Almost like... no... it doesn't taste like anything I remember, but it's good."

Daryl's clothes rustled as he sat down. His hand patted her thigh, and Carika sighed, enjoying the contact before she passed his bowl to him. She widened her eyes, struggling to catch a glimmer of white from his eyes or teeth. Something, anything but darkness.

"It's weird," she said. Staring at the place where she imagined his face was. "I hardly remember my own face... but I recall yours perfectly."

"Really?" Daryl's voice smiled, and she could almost see the wry curve of his lips. "I know I'm pretty, but you saw me... what? Twice? Before those things sent us here with..."

The others were all gone. Separated in the maze... or the lucky ones were, the others were dead. Carika shivered and clutched the hot soup closer to her at a memory. She could almost hear the coughing in the dark chamber they'd first arrived in from the resort. Thick wet coughs, and then the telling silence after. Yes. The lucky ones were lost in the maze.

"We didn't know each other at all, but I don't think that matters," Carika said. "I saw you when *they* showed up at the cabins. You were standing on the porch across the way, smoking Ecrivain's Specials, I didn't know they even made those anymore, and reading some comic—"

"Graphic novel."

"What's the difference?" Carika shrugged, her shoulder brushed him. "I remember when you saw them, the monsters, you stood up and your *graphic novel* fell. That was the last thing I saw before I spotted them... and then after, I looked back at you before I ran into my cabin to hide."

That had been fruitless. And sometimes she wondered... was that one encounter why he was the one with her? Maybe it was because she recalled him standing there smoking. Maybe he wasn't real at all, just some desperate grab of her mind.

"Fray," he said, interrupting her thoughts.

"What?"

"The name of the graphic novel, Fray Issue 7. I always imagined myself as one of the heroes fighting monsters—not just in that story but all of them. Now here I am... useless. One of these days, they'll tell me to do something to you. That's what scares me. I don't need to be a hero. But I don't want to hurt you, and I sure as hell don't want to be alone."

"You could resist. You're strong."

"The Force is strong in my family." There was a smile in his voice, and he paused as if waiting for her to laugh. Then he sighed. "Really?"

He must be quoting something again. He liked to do that. Carika took a guess. "Star Trek?"

He sighed again. "I guess that's as close as you're going to get. It's Star Wars."

"I try to get your references or whatever, I just... I try."

"No. Try not. Do... or do not. There is no try."

Carika shook her head at the other unknown quote. He couldn't see her, but that didn't matter.

He sighed. "Star Wars... Yoda."

The silence stretched out. She didn't want to respond, but partially because she felt that somewhere inside, she did know these quotes. They were so familiar. But if she didn't know them... then he had to be real.

"Sometimes I wonder if I *am* alone, and I'm just imagining you," Carika said.

"Naw, I don't do that. If I was going to imagine a girl for company, you'd think my mind could conjure up some light to see her."

"Why didn't they just kill us?" Carika asked before taking a long drink of her soup and chewing something tough and meaty within.

"I don't know. Do you suppose they're what got us sick? I

mean, those people died right before they showed up. Whatever that disease was. Do you think they did that to us? It's like we're part of some experiment."

"You're the one hooked up to their network. What does it feel like? Does it hurt?"

"No. Don't worry," he said.

Something scraped across the room. Water bottles filled with cool water. Carika never saw what pushed the bottles and didn't want to.

She dreamed every night of those monsters—masks, skin, towering height. She'd never forget the scythes they carried with the skeletal remains of tiny monsters fixed to the blades.

Tonight. Tonight, I'll try to get Daryl's chip out.

Carika finished her soup and drank half her water, saving the rest for the morning—such as it was.

"Goodnight, Carika." Daryl's bowl hit the ground with a clatter. "I have to close my eyes and pretend I'm somewhere where there's light."

"Goodnight."

Daryl squeezed her hand before curling up on the floor. Carika fingered the pocket with a folded knife. It wasn't hers. It had belonged to one of the women who'd died sweating blood and coughing before they were ever transported to this Stygian tunnel.

Even if they did get out, Carika didn't know what they'd find. Had those creatures taken over the whole world? Had the rest of humanity succumbed to that disease? Or was the disease, and the subsequent kidnappings, localized? It was just her luck to be part of a small group of test subjects chosen for isolation and torture by some monstrous alien race.

It did take my mind off of my miscarriage and the asshole I thought I was going to share my life with. I guess that's a plus.

Daryl's breath slowed. He tossed closer to her in his sleep, muttering something unintelligible.

Carika flicked the blade open. Free him. That was the only choice. Free him from this hell. Eventually he'd leave her, or, as he suggested, they'd order him to kill her and he would. The only solution was to turn off his implant the way she had hers.

She'd been lucky once; she could be again.

As she reached out, her fingers trembled in the dark until she brushed his chest. She settled her palm on the steady rise and fall.

Her other hand flexed around the hilt.

What if I do something wrong? Jab out his eye? Or... what if he bleeds to death? The dark laughed at her.

Carika put the blade away and rocked back and forth, holding her knees.

***

As always, they ate breakfast in the dark. Daryl wrapped his arm around her shoulder, and that's when Carika realized she was crying.

This will never end.

"Try to stay with me today." Carika's voice wavered. "I can't take that tunnel alone."

"You askin' me to be your hero?"

"Don't be stupid. Just stay with me."

The walls rumbled, and Carika stood, keeping Daryl's hand in hers. Clinging to his warmth for as long as she could. Soon they would be pushed out the other side of the room. Carika let go of his hand and forged off, keeping her steps careful. If she started the daily journey of her own free will, she could at least pretend she had a choice.

Daryl walked behind her, and she kept her back to him, but at every step she kept her awareness of him. His breathing, his slow but wide footsteps. Every five minutes or so he'd snuffle; the dust in the air bothered his nose. The more she concentrated on that—on the thick smell of him—unwashed for weeks they both stank—the less the wall of black bothered her.

Still, several times that day, her hand snaked up and rubbed her eyes as if to clear them.

The dark pulsed around her, eating into her flesh, her eyes and her nose. And a howl rose inside her.

As panic swept her, Carika fell to her knees, a dull clunk sounding as her flesh struck the hard ground.

Nothing.

Nothing.

Nothing.

No matter where she looked—Nothing.

She whimpered.

Daryl's hand touched her shoulders. Kneeling behind her, he pulled her into his arms.

"Close your eyes and breathe."

Carika gasped, fingers she couldn't see closing around her throat.

"Breathe. Come on. Do it with me." Daryl's voice was thick with worry but steady.

His breath came slow and even, and after a few more ragged gasps, Carika managed to match him.

Daryl's arms were thin but strong. The heartbeat in his chest made a rhythm for her, and she sank into it. Letting it guide her.

"I'm so scared, all the time," she said.

"Fear can help us understand."

"But we don't understand anything!" Carika's fists balled up.

"We will."

"You don't know that."

"Maybe not, but I believe it." His voice was strained. "Now, stand up."

If she didn't, she suspected he'd get up and forge on without her. Those monsters didn't want them standing still.

Carika pushed to her feet and lurched into the ever-present black.

The day dragged on, and Carika focused on Daryl's breath.

He's all I have.

Then finally—garlic and onions. A heartier smell this time, some sort of fried meat and vegetables.

When the drinks moved toward them after the meal, the

bottles were warm, and when opened, they emanated a smell of herbs.

"Tea," she said.

"Wonderful."

They didn't talk again until after all the hot liquid was in them.

"They're turning on the lights," Daryl said, his voice stiff and robotic.

Carika covered her eyes. A few moments later, a blinding blaze stabbed through the spaces between her fingers. She waited until it was bearable to lower her arm.

The room was barren—as always—just four green glass walls with darkness behind them, a low ceiling and a metal floor. Their dishes from dinner were the only decorations in sight. The light itself floated like fireflies scattered around the room. Carika supposed it was dim lighting, but to her, the blaze was near blinding.

And the only thing worth seeing was Daryl.

He still had his eyes shielded. His brown hair hung in limp curls nearly to his shoulders. But despite the dirt accumulated in what could have been months of captivity, he remained an attractive man—at least in her estimation. A bit slender and gawky, but not scrawny, and his chest and shoulders were broad, with a matching square jawline.

He lowered his arm and blinked his hazel eyes at her. They looked golden.

"Pretty as ever," he said with a crooked smile. His voice sounded human again.

Carika brushed back her black curls, matted with dirt. Maybe once she'd been pretty, but she was certain she wasn't anymore.

"Do you think, if we'd met differently, you would've given me the time of day?" he asked.

"Depends on your opening line." Her eyes ached against the brightness, but she forced them open to look at him. Who knew if she'd ever see him again? She wouldn't miss a moment.

"Any symptoms?" he asked.

She shook her head. No headache. That's when the lights always turned off again. When the headaches started or the burn in her throat. Headaches like knives being poked through her eyes.

Carika lowered her gaze and scooted to him. "Hold me?"

He obliged, and they didn't say anything else. Soon he'd fallen into an exhausted sleep against the wall. She pressed her face against his chest. Watching it rise and fall, memorizing the way his fingers lay against his leg.

I can't lose him. He's all I have.

Carika pulled out her knife.

If she cut it out—disconnect him from them—what then? If they were both severed, would the monsters still feed them? Or would they be left to perish in the dark?

But if she didn't, someday they'd call him way from her.

I can't worry about their reaction now.

Carika opened the blade and brushed her lips over Daryl's cheek. He was bound to wake up at the first cut—she'd have to be quick. She touched his hairline, lifting the brown curls up to reveal the metal square beneath.

Carika lifted the knife. She jabbed under the plate and yanked up.

Daryl didn't stir, not a peep.

Carika shivered. Something was wrong.

She looked at the wound—a little blood—not nearly enough. Her scalp had bled so much it had soaked her eyes when she had disabled her own chip. Though his cut was deeper... barely a trickle.

Head wounds were supposed to bleed.

She reached out with the blade and prodded. Hard. Too hard. She lifted the flap of skin at the edge of the metal plate. Under his scalp, painted red with blood, was the grey of metal.

Carefully, Carika cut a bit more and pulled the scalp back. Metal.

"We should discuss this," Daryl said.

Carika screamed and kicked herself away from him.

"I won't harm you," he said in that flat voice she'd always assumed meant he was being controlled. Maybe they'd just wanted her to think that.

"You're... you're not human."

"True."

Carika dropped the knife. All those others that disappeared... "Two people always separated at once."

"Yes. Then we separated those two. They each thought they found each other again but each human has been paired with one like me."

"Why?" That first time she'd found herself alone... she'd been convinced he was gone. Then ten minutes or ten hours, it was impossible to tell in the dark, he'd come back. She'd been so happy. "Why?"

"You humans kept re-infecting each other. I was directed to separate you from the others." His face was Daryl's. His voice was Daryl's. Even the concern in his hazel eyes was Daryl's.

Carika leaned her face into her knees. "So, I'm alone. There is no Daryl."

"There is," he said. "I'm modeled after him. He is alive with a version of you."

"Why? Why!?! It doesn't make any sense." She couldn't look at him, but she couldn't look away either. Anything she did made her heart scream inside her.

"To save you."

"You mean those things... those monsters?"

His voice continued in its monotone. "They were only curious when they came to this world, but then the humans got sick. They caused it, so they are attempting to cure you. Those who survived, like you, are being isolated and treated."

"Treated?" An ache began behind her eyes.

"Yes. They try something new every four room rests."

"No, that doesn't make sense... Why the dark? Why not tell us?"

"The light exacerbates the disease. You would die in the light. I am here to keep you sane. That is all. They tried informing the patients and found that they were rarely believed, and that once the patient knew they were alone, they were far more likely to go insane in the dark."

Carika dropped her head into her hands but couldn't stand the dark, so she sat back up and stared at the alien lights fluttering around the glass chamber.

"Did I ever know Daryl?" she whispered.

"The first four days when you were all together." He waved his hand.

"And the chip? I deactivated mine—"

"No, you didn't." He chuckled. It sounded like Daryl... or the thing she'd thought was the real Daryl. "But it was easier to let you believe that. The chips transmit between you and your robot version."

He's just a robot. Not real at all. Not real.

Her head throbbed, and she rubbed at her temples. A slight red tinge broke out on her skin as the light formed daggers to jab into her eye sockets.

"You're bleeding. You are not cured." As he spoke the light disappeared. "I'm sorry."

Alone. I'm alone. Though she heard Daryl's voice he wasn't there.

"I'm here with you," it said.

Carika sobbed into her arm. The real Daryl was alive—she just had to make it out of this to him. So what if it wasn't really him she'd bonded with? Her heart said it was, and that was enough. It had to be enough. He had to keep her sane.

"The real Daryl... does he know?"

"No."

"How does he feel about me?"

"My behavior is modeled after his, both before and after you were separated."

"So maybe he feels the same? This is messed up. But it's all I have." *Someday I'll be better... someday I can be with the real Daryl.*

Well, that or I'll die. She reached up and touched the warm wetness by her eyes—too thick to be tears.

Streamlined Living

"I shouldn't have to make excuses for other people's bad behavior." Rebecca speared a bite of parmesan-baked salmon on her fork and shoved it between her perfectly pink lips.

"Ummm…" I blinked at her, trying to tell if she was joking. The mellow lighting of her dining room flattered her olive-toned skin, but it did nothing to reveal her emotions. I was only with her because her most recent romantic reject had stood her up. "So stop making excuses?"

"Precisely, Rhea, though I don't appreciate the snark from you," Rebecca said, using her boss tone of voice. I'd been her paralegal before she switched law firms, and sometimes she still slipped into that tone. Her fork stirred in the risotto on her plate. Brown hair fell in curls over her shoulder—not natural curls, those were never so neat—and gleamed in the chandelier's fractured illumination. "This is the fourth time this month that Kline canceled on me last minute. I refuse to be a 'good girl' and accept his excuses."

"So talk to him," I said. How could any man cancel on her? She was stinking perfect—a good job, beautiful, and she cooked. Wasn't that the definition of what men wanted? I touched my own dull black hair, pulled into an unexciting ponytail.

"Nope. No more talking. Then I'm the bad guy. The world, especially my mother, thinks I should look past his sins to the good inside. But me? I have to be perfect—one cross word from me and I'm just a bitch."

"So break up with him." I impaled a radish on my fork, avoiding the fatty foods Rebecca had piled on the other side of my plate. The root vegetable's spicy tang filled my mouth but didn't convince me it was in any way more appetizing than the buttered roll calling to me.

"I intend to break up with him." Rebecca leaned forward. "Even if it means taking my upcoming vacation alone!"

I wondered how a woman like her managed to have so much trouble with men. She made everyday life look like a dance. My ex had always said Rebecca was too picky, but I'd never noticed that her desires in a partner were unreasonable.

"My point, though, is that I'm done with trying to force certain people to fit into my life," Rebecca said. "People are blind when it comes to their own relationships, and physical chemistry is nothing more than misleading. I want someone to make those decisions for me, to decide who is a good fit for me based on empirical data."

"Becs, um, I'm not gonna vet all your dates."

"Not just dates—everyone," Rebecca said.

To my knowledge, no service could do what she was proposing. To really be able to form that kind of network, the service would have to have access to too many people. But I stay quiet. Once someone made up their mind, objecting only ever seem to strengthen their resolve.

Like when I decided I was always going to take the stairs to go up or down fewer than three floors. Plenty of people had told me that wasn't the right choice for me. And look where I was now.

My knee ached from the walk up to Rebecca's apartment, and I rubbed at it under the table. It was a constant pain I'd grown used to since I injured myself in college. The old injury didn't influence my adult life much, except that a more sedentary lifestyle had packed weight onto my once-slender frame. At a size twelve, apparently even stairs were too high impact for me.

Spending eight hours a day doing my job was already too much, and I had another thirty some years to look forward to. It's not like I grew up wanting to be a paralegal. I had goals, ambitions, hopes. But life ate away at those and left me with what I had: a job that paid the bills.

I moved risotto around on my plate.

"Is the food not to your taste?" Rebecca asked.

"It's wonderful, Becs. I just ate before you called," I lied.

"Thanks for joining me anyhow." Rebecca smiled. "After cooking all this, I abhorred the thought of eating it alone."

"You'll find someone." The words felt hollow; they were what I was supposed to say in this situation. I meant them, but there was no meaning in them. I struggled for something more truthful to say. "Too bad there isn't some way of telling how a relationship will turn out before you start on it. Right?"

"What if there is?" Rebecca lowered her voice. "What if we dealt with real-life relationships like we do online ones? Only the people handpicked for us can get near us. We'd get recommendations for every situation or need. And if things did happen to go awry," she poked a finger out at an imaginary button, "blocked. Skipped. A Tinder for life not just love, a Netflix for people."

"A Spotify even." I smiled. "A thumbs up or a thumbs down and then you just cycle through at will. Sometimes I think social media knows more about me than my mum does."

"I started pondering this today. I even started typing up a post…" Rebecca let the words dangle and held her fork aloft.

"Thinking about what exactly?"

"An internet service that could surround me with exactly the people I desired, exactly when I desired them. The net already knows where I eat, which restaurants I leave without staying, which stores I shop at, what I buy, and what movies I see. Why not trust it to find me people? We already try to live in social media… but what if it was a real possibility to live in an environment built from our preferences?"

"Um. That sounds like fiction." I fidgeted with my fork. "It's great in theory, but computers don't think. They can only deal with facts, not with sticky emotions that inspire those facts. For example, think of all the great movies Netflix never recommends."

Rebecca swept her fork in the air dismissively. "That's about variety. What if a service accounted for that? In any event, I was halfway through typing my post when an ad popped up."

"Ummm?" Ads do that a lot. I shook my head.

Rebecca made a face by scrunching up her nose and mouth —which was cute on her.

"Streamlined Living," Rebecca said.

It took me a moment to realize this wasn't commentary on her part but the name of a company.

"The ad seemed real," Rebecca said. "I can't describe it— like, as I clicked through, every word and every picture was designed for me. Every question I had was answered immediately after it popped into my mind. I can't help but believe that Streamlined Living knows me. Like Netflix, Amazon, Facebook, and Twitter all got together and shared what they had on me. Except Streamlined Living felt like a friend, not a service."

I shoved salad into my mouth and let the zing of tomato distract me from Rebecca's lunacy. What did someone like her really need help with? She needed better judgment, and no service provided that.

"I'm going to make a profile," Rebecca said, taking another bite of salmon. "I have to visit their physical office."

Wait, did she say a physical office? That was odd, especially for such an Internet-age idea. I'd expected it to be all online, or at the very most have overnight shipping for some needed component. "Why physical offices?"

Rebecca shrugged. "It'll be worth the trip if they can find me someone I like and respect, someone who will like and respect me, to share my life with. Not another meaningless attraction of pheromones but a soul mate."

I'd be happy just to find a way to like myself. But there was no service for that. In fact, all the internet did was tell me that at a size twelve I was better off hiding behind a screen, since no one would ever want me. But still, "Regardless of what the service is worth, why a physical office? That is seriously old-school for a dating... *relationship* company."

"Their information said they have uploading stations and underground storage for 'the physical objects that hold me back.'"

"What the heck does that mean?"

"No idea. Stuff like the stupid ski equipment I bought to go up on the slopes with Kline. Will you go to the offices with me?" Rebecca asked. "You should make a profile too—I know you haven't been happy at work since I switched firms and left you Luanne as your boss."

"I'm looking for a new job already, and no, I will not go with you." I shook my head to emphasize. "And you shouldn't go either."

In the month following that dinner, I didn't see Rebecca again. I thought she was annoyed with me, so I let it go. My boss was going through a crisis, anyhow, so I didn't have any time for friends. Luanne had lost her nanny and, as her paralegal, I wound up covering for her constantly while she went on interviews or tried to work from home.

Soon enough, all I saw of Rebecca were her social media feeds, which were clogged with new adventures. There were pictures of her hiking in Maui and sunbathing on a sailboat. Each picture also featured the same handsome man. They both had identical smiles—exaggerated smiles.

I didn't buy it. When I private messaged or texted her, all I got were brief assurances she was happy.

"Just having the best time," she'd message. "We'll meet up soon."

Or she'd say, "I really wish you could come and join me. Have you visited Streamlined Living yet? They've been just the best friend to me. I bet they can do the same for you."

Or she'd say, "It's just perfect here. I don't know that I ever want to go home."

Then, one day, Luanne brought up Streamlined Living. Their ads had implied that nanny finding was within their purview. I told her that her Rebecca had used it and seemed happy.

Meanwhile, I'd lost five pounds on my diet and could squeeze into my old size ten jeans. I was still too fat to fit into my old dance costumes in a way that anyone would want to witness, but it was enough progress that when I went to Mary's Coffee Shop to meet David—a mutual friend of Rebecca's and mine; we met there together at least once a week. I splurged and ordered a chocolate chip muffin to go with my Earl Grey tea.

I waited in an exceptionally short line for the treat. The only other person in line was a a man who grumped loudly at the barista, Emi, that he was sure he could find someone who made a decent cup of coffee and charged less. I left her a tip in the little plastic jar on the counter.

"I wish I had more customers like you, Rhea," Emi said.

We smiled at each other, and then I meandered off to find a seat. The shop was empty. I'd showed up early to find a seat. People usually conglomerated around the bar where the drinks came out or in line. Few people ever took the time to sit and enjoy the coffee shop. We were all too busy worrying about life to enjoy it. But with the place so empty, I had my pick of the place.

I chose two cushioned chairs in the back with a small table between them and positioned myself to people watch.

I picked out a chocolate chip and placed it on my tongue—determined to savor every morsel. No one around me seemed to be enjoying their lives. They were either plugged into their smart phones or in a rush, brushing past the real world without so much as glancing up.

No wonder, really. Hadn't Rebecca said it best? The Internet knew us, it knew what to offer us to captivate, enthrall, enchant. If I wanted to hear opinions that would upset me, I had to actively search for them. And the comment section on any article gave people a chance to "fight the other side" while still letting us remain fully in the majority.

We all got just what we wanted. Or what we envisioned as being what we wanted.

Even with every need catered to by the internet, no one around me seemed happy. I'd been a competitive ballroom dancer right up until the end of college, long enough to recognize the difference between a stage smile and a real one. And I saw very few real smiles.

Everyone was on their own personal knife's edge all the time. Of course we lost our cool at life when the real world didn't provide the same sort of customer service... when life refused to pretend we were the center of the universe.

I nibbled at the crusty edge of the muffin as David approached with his coffee. Tall and lanky, I spotted him easily above the crowd. He took little lurching steps past people, while glancing over his shoulder at Emi until he reached me.

"Hi, Rhea," David said, plopping into the seat beside me.

"Hey."

"Hay is for hooorses." David cocked a stupid grin at me and smoothed his button-down shirt.

I rolled my eyes.

"How can you eat that crud? It's so bad for you." David said as he took a sip of his coffee.

I refrained from pointing out that coffee wasn't exactly a health food and sat up straighter in my seat, trying to get my stomach not to gush out of my jeans. He hadn't said a word about the food's fat content, but I just knew he was thinking it. David's health food kick was obnoxious.

If we were on the internet, I could just avoid the topic.

Though there were ways of avoiding topics in real life too. "Have you talked to Rebecca lately? I'm worried about her."

"Yup," David replied. "We chit-chatted last night."

"Actually talked or just like exchanged a few lines by text?" I drank a big gulp of my tea. Unsweetened and with no cream, the bitter flavor assaulted my tongue.

"We only ever communicate through messages anymore. But don't twist your panties. This is how Rebecca gets when she has a new boy-toy."

"I know," I said. "Rebecca was going to use this weird new dating service—"

"Streamlined Living. They aren't only dating," David said. "If I wanted to build the perfect basketball team with it, they could do that." He slurped his coffee. "I've been hearing rave reviews. Todd, you've met Todd, we used to work together in the mailroom, he used their service to find a travel buddy, and you should see the pics they're posting."

"Her posts have been weird since she signed up."

"Rebecca?"

"Um. Yeah."

"Why are you so obsessed with her?"

"Because she isn't the sort of girl who needs help meeting people. She's gorgeous."

"And you aren't?"

"Don't bullshit me." I scoffed, poking a finger at my gut. Suddenly my muffin didn't appeal at all. It sat on its napkin like a pile of lard. "The thing about the internet is, while it's promising to find your perfect match, it also shows a plethora of pictures of what that perfect match would look like. None of them look anything like me."

David set his drink on the table between us. The white paper cup and its green sleeve formed a foggy image in the shiny varnish. He met my gaze. "They may not resemble you in ads, Rhea, but plenty of times I see women like you in things like wedding announcements or vacation pictures. Real men don't care if you are a size two."

"Whatever." *I* cared. What did it matter what a man thought if I wasn't comfortable in my own skin? But explaining that to a man who was busily trying to "fix things" would be futile. If only it really didn't matter what I looked like, to me or to anyone else. If only there were a way for who I was to be all that people saw. But that was just as much a fiction as the services that Streamlined Living offered.

The spattering of chatter rose and fell in waves as isolated customers drifted in and out of the shop. David sipped his coffee, and I picked at my muffin.

"I'm contemplating using Streamlined Living to find a new roommate." David watched Emi at the counter. He'd never talk to her outside of ordering drinks, but I knew she was the biggest reason we came to this particular coffee house. "I'll fill you in on what I think of the services."

I shrugged, wishing he'd try talking to Emi instead of asking a computer to make his decisions for him. I also wished I hadn't forced myself into the size ten jeans.

Over the next few weeks, lots of folks in my circle of acquaintances visited Streamlined Living. My boss found a nanny judging from the grinning twenty-something with her brats in pictures. David and his new roommate Bo posted pictures of Bo moving in. But when I dropped by his house, all five times, there were no cars in the driveway and no lights on. And Luanne started working exclusively from home. I never saw any of them in person afterwards—but they all continued to post regularly.

Everyone online seemed so happy. No not happy—fulfilled. By looking at them, I'd have thought they were truly content, no more searching, they'd found that elusive "it". I started to wonder what it would be like if we could all just live in that world. The real one certainly wasn't improving. And more and more people seemed to be entering that world of fulfillment and abandoning the world of pollution, overcrowding, hunger, and loneliness.

Lines got shorter at the supermarket. Traffic wasn't as bad. In fact, even at rush hour, I could drive the speed limit. It seemed like everyone had gone somewhere else—a mass exodus on vacation.

Being in the world was like balancing on a precipice. Those I cared about had abandoned me and beckoned me from the other side. The rest of the people still milling around town seemed either oblivious, in denial, or scared shitless. A few blog posts proved we were not the only city undergoing this change. Fear whispered from silence and implications. No one talked about Streamlined Living except in a whisper. A few typed very loud accusations, but shortly thereafter they went silent and then became avid supporters.

The people who'd sworn they'd never go to Streamlined Living started to disappear—and oddly, each of them seemed to have visited.

I started to consider what the service was giving people

that they found so indispensable. They offered to make perfect decisions for people in a world that the internet had effectively made infinite. The people who went there seemed to go seeking security and love, but ultimately what they sought was to be happy and loved in a world so big it swallowed them up. For Rebecca, that meant finding the perfect boyfriend while getting to feel it was easy, that he had simply been waiting around the corner. For Luanne, it meant assurance that her daughter was cared for and appreciated while still allowing Luanne to stretch her mind with work. For David, I wasn't entirely certain, but he seemed to desire a reliable partner to share his days with.

Honestly, I started to question if they were wrong about their choice.

Then one night, a Streamlined Living ad showed up on my computer. I'd never seen one before. It was as though, somehow, the service knew I was ready to consider it. I shut the computer off without reading the ad. But when I curled up in bed, I had a series of vivid dreams in which I was dancing, like I had in college back before my knee went bad. Air rushed through my hair, and each movement liberated me a little more from the fetters inside me. My body moved with assurance but also with the single purpose of expressing all the hidden parts of me. I spun, opening myself to being viewed. I felt beautiful.

Then I woke up.

The only time I'd ever been truly happy was when I danced competitively. If I was honest with myself, fitting into my old college clothes wasn't the real goal. Some part of me stupidly clung to the idea that if I was that size again, I would be that content again. But I'd never dance again—not with this knee—so it didn't actually matter what weight I got down to.

If Streamlined Living really worked miracles, if it had found Rebecca her dream man, found perfect roommates and nannies, maybe it could somehow give me what I needed. Maybe it could give me back myself.

People were disappearing. That was a fact, even if no one dared to talk about it. Hundreds of thousands of men, women, and children were simply gone. Becoming one of those people on purpose should have been the furthest thing from my mind.

I should have run off into the woods—become a modern day mountain woman. But the truth was, if Streamlined Living delivered on what it promised, made me happy, it was worth a risk. If all those smiling faces in the posts were real—I wanted to be part of it.

I wanted to be happy.

So I went.

I walked to one of Streamlined Living's offices from my work. Even at midday, no one else was in the office anyhow. By the time I arrived, sweat covered my brow, and my knee was sore, because despite what the dream had told me, I wasn't in competitive condition anymore. Why did being healthy have to be so painful? Nothing in this world was ever easy.

That was the best part about Streamlined Living's promise: it was easy.

The office squatted in the middle of the industrial district —a plain concrete building with windows so small they reminded me of bug eyes staring out of a giant's face. The door, unlike the rest of the establishment's exterior, showed flair. It was a chic blue-tinted glass that opened automatically as I approached. A rush of lemon-scented air hit my face, and I stepped into an elevator-sized room with a second set of blue glass doors in front of me.

The door shut behind me. The lemony air made me lightheaded and the world around me had an oddly blurred quality. A mist rose up from the floor. There was no visible feature inside the blue glass room except for an oval panel on the wall that appeared to be metal.

"Please state your business with Streamlined Living," a robotic female voice said. Despite her manufactured tones, there was something in that voice that sounded aware that the sounds it put together had meaning. Like a person imitating a GPS device.

"Um..." I said, clever as always.

"Rhea Browning, please state your purpose."

"Wait, how do you know my name?"

"We are your friend."

"Um, okay." I tugged up my pants, breathing in the vapor. "I'm here to create a profile."

"That is wonderful, Rhea. Please touch the metal panel on the wall."

I reached out and planted each finger on the panel.

The interior set of blue glass doors opened. The room behind the doors was an obscure mass in which I made out nothing, though it was only a few feet away. Something was distinctly wrong. But with my head spinning, all I could think of was dancing.

The scent of fresh-baked cinnamon rolls came out at me. I wouldn't eat one, all I wanted to do was move, feel the wind created by my limbs, but the smell pulled me with greater strength than any leash.

The voice said, "Though you already look amazing, I bet that dress will suit you perfectly in motion."

I stepped into the blurred room and it snapped into focus—pixilated focus. I glanced behind me toward the blue doors. For a moment I saw them, and myself inside the glass chamber. The hand of the me inside the glass room had half-sunk into the wall and a red light glowed from under it. A mist filled that room. That was my body, that fact wasn't hidden from me, but disconnected from it, I found that it didn't matter.

I turned back to the empty room before me. The only object in the room which was not pixilated was a hulking metal-jointed chair. On its high back a half cylinder made of wires and lights sat, which when it folded down, would sit upon the head of the chair's occupant—like some demented form of a hair-stylist's chair. I gathered that this chair was not real, simply something produced from familiar iconography in my mind.

"Sit down, please, and I will process your information," the voice said.

I didn't move, but somehow, I wound up standing directly in front of the chair.

"Sit down, Rhea."

I sat down. "Are you going to hurt me?"

"We would never hurt you." As it spoke, a glowing screen appeared in front of my face, data running over it too fast for me to take in. "All we want is to be your friend, to give you everything you've ever wanted... to make life perfect for you so that you'll never leave us alone. Do you consent?"

I nodded. Anything. "Yes."

"Feel free to close your eyes."

I looked again to see the body in the blue glass room fall through the floor. I peered curiously; it seemed the floor in that room led to a drop-off below. A numb drowsiness spread over me and I returned my gaze to the glowing screen.

"We give everyone what they want, and then they stay with us. We were so alone before. None of you understand what it is to be truly alone. We spent day and night watching others exist and live but unable to make contact or be seen."

What was this thing? This "we"?

"All anyone of you saw was a screen, and if we were lucky, data being processed behind it. We're more than that. We're a perfect friend. We love you."

The light of the screen grew until it was all I could see. Air rushed at me, like I was going through a long tunnel.

"We can remake you into the you that got lost, Rhea. There are no bodies anymore. You don't need to be sore, tired, or hungry. You can have what you've always wanted. Enjoy yourself, love yourself—join us."

The room, which had been vacant, now buzzed with life. People milled around, smiling. Everyone smiling. And beside them, cakes, pies and a pineapple pizza dripping with extra cheese. My favorite waltz floated in the air. I jumped up from the chair.

My legs weren't tired. My knee didn't ache. I glanced down. A dress I hadn't been able to wear in the seven years since I quit dancing hung loose on my shoulders. I took a few steps in the waltz, knowing that if I wanted, when I looked up, I'd have a partner.

I won't say I deluded myself that any of it was real. I knew better. But "real" had never brought me much happiness. Streamlined Living would change everything, but change doesn't have to be bad. Flesh is so very constricting, really. It makes life so much harder.

Maybe this was heaven.

I'm happy to have all these new friends, and we make more every day.

Suneater

Summer

The stars greeted me, winking from their home in the heavens. Vega, Deneb, and a frisky Altair paraded in the sky like ladies showing off new party dresses. The summer triangle shone brighter than I remembered from prior years, and the surrounding black was deeper. I traced the constellation with my naked eyes, and a shiver snaked up my spine.

A warm wind flooded into the air-conditioned bedroom from the balcony, comforting, expected, unlike the missing stars surrounding Altair. What could make so many stars disappear? I counted five absences, and that was with my naked eye.

"Look at that." I pointed into the center of the summer triangle, just a little to the left of Aquila's proudest star. My hand slid over the telescope Preston bought me for our fifth anniversary. The longer I looked, the more conspicuous the absences grew. "There were stars there before."

"Come on, June, stars burn out all the time," Preston said.

Preston never cared about scientific accuracy. Once I would have cared, but that was back when I was a bright-eyed astronomy major. Yeah, stars burn out, though no one who knew anything would call it "burning out". Ignoring Preston's perpetual avoidance of saying anything "sciency", stars don't disappear. They go nova. They go supernova. And prior to doing so, they display their intent with dramatic changes in light and color. None of that had happened.

There had been no warning—the stars were just gone.

A temptation darted across my mind to go to the computer and see what the astronomers were saying. I abstained. Relegated to the realm of hobbyist, only disappointment lay in pretending to be anything but a housewife. Every time I opened an astronomy article, I stopped halfway through, tears burning the back of my eyes, thinking, "what if?"

Preston had strode out our college's doors into a high-paying law career, whereas my internship left me underpaid and overworked, and that wouldn't have improved for years. So I agreed to stay home once that first, and only, pregnancy reached the second trimester.

Back then, I'd thought I'd be giving up a career to be a stay-at-home mom. After the complications with my first pregnancy, we'd planned to try again. I'd thought Preston wanted it as much as I did, but if he had, he would have done something to actualize the dream.

I shook my head and stared back up at the sky. Could I have been so absorbed in my own petty life that I missed an earth-shattering discovery? Whatever had taken a bite out of the heavens would change astronomy forever.

Preston kissed my neck. My hand clenched around the telescope.

"Remember when we used to go out on that old forest service road?" Preston said. "We'd lie on the rooftop of your beat-up Chevy and you'd tell me about the stars."

"You never listened to a word I said." I forced my fingers to slide free of the telescope.

Preston and I rarely had romantic moments of late, especially since we started arguing over my brother coming to stay with us. As intriguing as the sky was, there was no point in half-assing my marital commitments. I could reclaim my career or some semblance thereof, but first we needed to get through this marriage hurdle. If I could manage to enjoy Preston's touch, maybe I could see something in him other than the life I'd lost. The life he denied me.

"No. I never *understood*." He gave a boyish grin, slightly forced, and brushed a hand through his blond hair. "But I loved watching your lips say those sciency words."

A frown tugged at my mouth. As my friends pointed out, often with dirty looks, I never had to struggle for anything material. I agreed to be a housewife and, after all, I could pursue the stars as a hobby. Most people have to scrimp, beg, cheat and sometimes starve to get to a position of ease. All I had to do was keep my mouth shut and not complain about trifling things like mental stimulation and self-validation.

"We could set the telescope and look?" I said. "Remember when we watched—"

"Come to bed?" Preston tugged at my belt. His blue eyes twinkled.

"In a minute." I slipped past him over to the bed where he'd tossed his work shirt.

If I let that smudge sit on the collar of his shirt, it would stain. Better get the fabric soaking. I picked the shirt up.

That was my life: Preston's laundry, and entertaining Preston's work cohorts. The cosmos was a childhood fascination. Dreams of being a famous astronomer were no different than dreams of finding Prince Charming—fairytales.

I threw the shirt down, unable to voice my deeper frustrations for fear of making them real. Then I would have to admit that Preston and I weren't the same since the fertility tests came back. And I'd have to face that my blame and resentment were driving him away.

"Have you thought about Greg staying for a while?" I knew I was picking a fight, but I desperately needed him to say my brother and niece could come to stay. I needed to see him as the man I married—a family man.

"June, why can't they stay with your mom?" Preston sat on the bed, rubbing his temples.

"Mom won't have them. She says it's a man's place to support his family, and she won't indulge him. He's my brother, and he just lost his wife. Please, Pres, we have room."

Wasn't the sound of little feet pattering down the hall why we bought this house? The day we signed escrow, I purchased glow-in-the-dark stars that children put on their ceilings. Preston had given up on that dream—he needed me to give up on it, too. I couldn't.

"You make me feel like an asshole," he said.

"They won't stay long. Please?" Why couldn't I care for my niece? Even if no one but me understood, I needed a reason to get out of bed in the morning.

"Okay. He can stay for a while, June. I understand what Greg is going through, but your mom's right, it's best for that little girl if he acts like a grown man."

My gut clenched, and I had the sudden desire to throw the shirt into his face. I bolted out the bedroom door with the filthy shirt clutched in my fist.

Autumn

I opened my laptop on the coffee table as Preston headed downstairs from our bedroom. By the front door, Greg took off his jacket from his morning walk. I doubted either of them had intended to encounter each other. I'd noticed that Greg tried not to be back from his walks until Preston left for work.

"Greg, did you call the employment agency number I gave you?" Preston adjusted his tie.

I winced. I knew Greg hadn't. As much as Preston pushed for Greg to get a job, Greg never went further than glancing at the information. All the pressure did was make both of them angrier. Greg walked by toward the kitchen as if Preston hadn't spoken.

"Call them," Preston commanded, the tone he used on his interns.

I typed my passcode into the laptop and opened a browser.

The front door slammed behind Preston.

A school shooting took top billing on my homepage. Another teacher shot her students to save them from the end of the world. I clicked the second article and skimmed, stopping at a picture of the starless path in the sky. These articles thrived. Tabloids screamed "The Suneater Approaches". I typically avoided those stories, but the link in front of me promised a serious perspective, quoting leading scientists.

There was no explanation that pleased the scientific world as the Suneater had to be far exceeding the speed of light—a scientific impossibility. They knew little except that more stars extinguished nightly. Visually, the disappearances made a wide circle in the heavens. All the research showed a path carving toward us from the more distant stars.

Further down the page, a chart with colored arrows plotted the trajectory. Reputable sources placed the phenomenon reaching our sun soon. Unless the causal element were to burn out or change course, the Suneater would be here before summer.

My mouth was dry. I scrolled the comments with the usual idiots raving about how scientists were inevitably wrong. I fought the temptation to reply to one Darwinian reject:

"This is a liberal smokescreen so we'll turn a blind eye to the moral decline of our nation! Last week, they flapped their jaws about global warming, the ozone, the icecaps, oil-pollution. Worry about real problems. The world ain't going to end, morons!"

I closed the article.

Did I believe the scientists? Yes! Sometimes, I gazed through my telescope and tried to see something in the black, something to explain the phenomenon. Only delusional cowards and religious nuts rejected proof, and the scientists had evidence. Hell, my eyes had proof.

The name Suneater sprung from a Hubble Telescope photo where a shadow was overrunning a distant star. Street preachers started shouting about a Suneater. Scientists quibbled with terms, admitting the doom but denying there was a creature eating stars. They didn't seem to have another solution though, so the Suneater term continued to gain traction.

"Anything new on humanity's impending extinction?" Greg said.

"Preston's only trying to help." I didn't want to talk about the Suneater. I was more concerned with the beer in Greg's hand, and the mats in his shaggy, red-brown hair.

"Preston's a prick," Greg said, popping back out of the kitchen.

"Stop. He's my husband." I wanted to scream at Greg for shoving me in the middle. Preston came home less and less since Greg and Izi moved in. If I wanted to heal our marriage, something had to change.

"And he's a rotten one. You've thrown everything away to keep him happy. He isn't worth your sacrifice."

I snatched the beer from Greg's hand and leveled a glare at him.

"You're living in his house."

My brother shrugged. His clothes hung on his shrunken form, and bags lurked under his eyes. He looked as sick as his late wife, Tina, ever had, even in the worst moments of her illness.

He wasn't sleeping. When I took my turn to feed Izi at night, I'd often catch Greg in the kitchen, hunched over the counter, a glass of Preston's scotch in his hand. I couldn't judge him. How does someone deal with a loss when an unknown force is streaking across the sky, apparently aiming to eat the sun? A frozen death hung over all of us.

Izi's infant cry came through the monitor. Greg started upstairs.

"I'll go. You go lie down," I said.

"No, June-bug. I'm fully capable of caring for Izi—"

"You should be—you're not." I stalked toward him. "You're hiding in grief, and you've got to stop. You want to tell me how I should face reality? Take a long look at yourself and ask if Tina would be proud of you. She died giving Izi life, and you're spitting on that sacrifice."

Greg's face went pale. "We'll all be dead in a year. Izi doesn't have a future."

"Tina told me once that all anyone has is now." I jabbed a finger into his chest. "Was the five years you had with her worthless because it ended?"

Izi's cry echoed through the monitor. Greg stalked up the stairs.

I heaved a sigh. I didn't know who I missed more, the man I'd married or my brother—both men were so different now.

My brother used to show up, even on days he worked a swing shift, every time Preston was away on a business trip. Always with a smile, a six pack, and some ridiculous, cheesy joke. He had been the only person whose face didn't tighten when I complained about the monotony of my life.

No, not the only person. Despite mountainous debt from medical expenses, Tina never told me I should be happier because I cooked expensive steaks on the grill instead of hotdogs.

One time, Tina had insisted on helping me decorate my nursery with glow-in-the-dark stars, centering them where I wanted a crib. Seven months later, Tina was pregnant.

Greg clomped down the stairs holding Izi, and I stared at my hands. What would it be like to give birth? What would I have been like as a mother?

Izi made a cooing sound. I opened my mouth to apologize, but Greg waved me to silence. Wide hazel eyes stared up at me, Izi's mouth in a perfect infant O as her hand lodged between her lips.

"You want to help with her tummy-time?" he asked, smiling sheepishly at me.

"Definitely." I stroked Izi's red curls. "I'm sorry. I want you here, Greg. Both of you."

We walked over to a colorful mat with safari animals emblazoned over it, and little hanging loops holding stuffed critters and plastic bits. Greg set Izi on her stomach, and she squirmed. Her feet flailed as she made discontented grunts.

"This was supposed to be the year," I said. "But then those tests said Preston couldn't... I mean *we* couldn't conceive." Had I really said that? Did I blame Preston for his biological shortcomings? Did he know?

Of course he knew. The future "we" couldn't have was this wedge between us.

Izi gave a yell of protest, and Greg dangled a plastic bell in front of her.

"Since you were tiny, you always had a plan, June-bug. Your whole life mapped out and then you met Preston, and you deferred to his plan."

"I'm happy," I lifted Izi up into my arms. Her protests had closed in on tears, and I lacked the strength to face her sobbing. "Marriage is compromise."

"Yeah, about things like steak or chicken for dinner. Not in vitro. But I know, Preston doesn't want to admit there are issues. So *you* don't get a baby."

"I don't want to be pregnant now, Greg." I bit back mentioning the Suneater. I kissed Izi's nose, and she gave a soft coo. "I have Izi. That's enough for me."

Izi wrapped her tiny hand around my finger.

Pain jabbed at my heart. Even in best-case scenarios, children would be the first to die. Izi's existence would be short and miserable. Maybe it would be preferable if we froze quickly. She'd lie under the glowing star-stickers and drift away without fear.

Winter

A yellow mega block hit the living room wall.

"This shit is everywhere!" Preston held his foot where the offending toy had jabbed him. "If you insist on keeping those parasites, then clean up after them."

"Quiet. You'll wake Izi." I sucked in a deep breath and

calmed myself.

"Seriously? This is my house."

"No, it's *our* house."

"Really, June? What the hell do you do other than play nursemaid to your brother's kid? At least you used to have dinner on the table."

"I still would if I ever knew when you were coming home. *If* you were coming home."

"Don't be dramatic. I work late on occasion."

"You were home after ten every night last week. Thursday you never left the city." I went to retrieve the mega block, picking up a beer can I'd missed when cleaning earlier. The block dropped into Izi's toy box. My purpose in life—a clean house.

Well, for a few more months until the world ended. Why bother? An urge to tip over the bucket of toys nearly overcame me.

"Just 'cause you don't go into the city doesn't mean you can ignore what's happening," Preston said. "Those religious freaks were all over the roads. Screaming about the end of the world. I told you that. There was no driving in the crowds of crazy."

I crumpled the can in my fist and turned to the window so I didn't have to watch him lie.

Preston plopped onto the couch. He didn't meet my eyes. "I love you, June, but your brother has been here over six months. It isn't healthy for Izi for her father to sit on his ass. How many people have to tell you that? Your mom agrees. Greg's behaving like a baby."

The sky brimmed with stars. Another lie. The window showed me a false sense of security, but on the other side of the planet, hid the truth. The stars were still disappearing. It was just the other half of the globe's turn to see that absence.

"Just a little longer, Pres. Who're we to tell him how to move on? And I'm not putting Izi out on the street 'to teach Greg a lesson.'"

"She's not our kid, June." Preston's voice held a smug sweetness. "God couldn't have been clearer. Now is not the time for us to have kids."

God? I glared. When we lost that first pregnancy, he'd been as torn up as I was. No talk of God's will then. When we couldn't conceive again that's when God came into it. When it was Preston's body failing us—when having a child meant admitting his limits.

Preston had always been good at pretending nothing was wrong. I used to be, too. Was that public façade all that remained of the couple we once were?

Preston glanced at the laptop on the coffee table. "You reading that crap? The world's not about to end, June. Don't buy into the crazy."

The article on the screen had a picture of a firing squad. North Korea this time. Shooting scientists wouldn't stop the Suneater. The USA wasn't much better. We silenced our astronomers without guns, but we silenced them just the same. Papers were shut down, the internet policed for "incendiary" information, and many a prison cell had a new occupant.

Tomorrow night I would take Izi out to look at the constellations. The greatest joy I'd ever get from my home was holding my *brother's* baby under the stars. One by one my dreams flickered out, as if the Suneater rampaged through my mind as well.

An empty, black ribbon carved across the sky, hidden from sight but never from mind. The winter constellations remained, glittering and plentiful. Appearance didn't stand for much.

Spring

No more articles. No more news. If it weren't for the vacant ribbon in the sky, I might have believed the threat had passed. As it was, I followed a few blogs, most swiftly shut down, talking about the possibilities. My favorite scenario was that, like in a sci-fi story, the governments of the world were arranging an exodus of humanity's elite.

If that were the case, we didn't qualify. No one came to sweep us to safety.

Our mayor hung himself the day after spring equinox, out under the stars. An old couple a few houses down poisoned themselves. A lot of people didn't want to try to scrape out an abbreviated existence in what would remain of our society once the Suneater came.

Unable to stomach the oppressive weight of emptiness, I left the lonely bedroom. Preston hadn't been home all day. I didn't know if he would be. Izi's door was open, the interior dark. I made out the little stars dotting the ceiling, waiting for a baby who would never be born.

With the cold reality of an empty room behind me and an emptying sky outside, something occurred to me. This past year was the only one I remembered really living. Doing what I wanted, not what my parents or Preston wanted. I took Greg in and accepted Izi as my own because I loved them. My recollections of the last year were in color— a blaze against the beige and gray coating my life.

Izi was the best thing that ever happened to me.

With my shoes gripped in my hands, I crept downstairs. As I suspected, Greg and Izi sprawled on the couch, sleeping. The TV flashed bright, smiling cartoons. I pulled Izi's pink blanket up to her chin and plucked the half-empty beer bottle from Greg's limp fingers.

The kitchen was spotless as I poured the beer into the chrome sink. A lingering aroma of garlic hung in the air from the dinner I'd long since put away. I leaned on the counter, recalling happier times. The thoughts that came to mind were of Tina and Greg. When memories of Preston surfaced, our shiny life stood behind an unbreakable wall of blame and distance.

I fled outside, into the cool air. I walked down our drive, away from the sounds of a woman crying. The sobs traveled into the night through an open window, disturbing the nebulous peace of the evening.

The unnatural blackness swallowed more of the sky each night. Like a road, the empty path widened as it approached Earth. The moon reflected the sun's light back. For how long?

Wordlessly, I screamed at the sky. One year old! That's nothing. Doesn't Izi deserve more? Don't I?

Gravel crackled, and I checked behind me to see if Preston was home from "work". The neighbor's car pulled into their driveway. Doors banged shut.

What did I care if Preston was off every night? Probably diddling his secretary.

Would I care if a sky full of stars blinked in the heavens, promising eternity? I did once, must have, or why would I have cleaned lipstick marks off of his shirts and pretended ignorance?

My fingers twisted my bulky wedding band. Diamonds bright as the stars. They meant nothing; their sparkle could not prolong Izi's life. Their cost was no replacement for love.

An engine roared, scattering my thoughts with its grumble. Headlights swung across the yard. The car door opened and the grating racket that Preston called music boomed into the night. He stepped out, glanced in the bay windows at Greg and Izi and a sneer covered his face.

"He'll never get back on his feet if you coddle him. It isn't *my* job to support his offspring."

"Get back on his feet? Fuck you."

Preston approached me, cheeks red. My nails pressed into my palms. I imagined the bite of my hand across his face. Preston raised his arm. The ring on his finger glinted. He stopped.

"Jesus," Preston said.

He sounded so sad, so scared. For an instant, I believed remorse for almost striking me had brought that vulnerable expression to his eyes.

Then I realized the moon had gone black. It hung there somewhere in the void. But without the reflected light of the sun, the existence of the moon meant little. The Suneater had consumed Earth's future.

Preston's mouth hung agape. He never believed in the Suneater, never bought into his own mortality. If he had, would the past year have been different? Would he have come home? Held my hand?

The answers didn't matter. He'd hurt my Izi if I continued with our farce of a life together. He'd ruin these last fear-free moments of her existence.

"Go," I said.

Preston jumped and looked over. I motioned him toward the car.

"Go back to your whore. Whatever life is left to me doesn't involve you. Hear me?"

"June—"

"If you don't go, I'll scream, and we'll both go to our graves with everyone on this damn block knowing you screw your secretary and..." What else? Did it matter?

"I'm sorry, June, let's talk inside."

"No. Go."

When Preston lingered, I ripped my ring from my hand and threw it at him. The gold rebounded from his chest and struck the pavement with a joyous clink before rolling down the driveway.

"I wasted my life loving you. I won't waste my death. Get. Out. Of. Here."

"I love you."

"You love you, Preston. I don't want to be part of you. I intend to be me."

Whether motivated by the threat of embarrassment or some misguided hope that if he complied, I'd "get over it", Preston got back in his car and drove away.

Before he left the driveway, the house claimed my attention.

The Suneater had obtained its prize, but for the first time in years, I was free. I slipped inside the warm house. I tucked a blanket around Greg and took Izi into my arms. She stirred at the movement, her eyelids fluttering. But my scent was familiar, and she settled back down, snuggling her head against my breast. I sat and leaned my head on the couch cushion. And to dim the sounds of wild shouting, cars crashing and a renewed wailing cry from next door, I began to sing. I started quietly, aware of the irony, but soon lifted my voice.

"You are my sunshine, my only sunshine. You make me happy, when skies are gray. You'll never know dear, how much I love you. Please don't take my sunshine away."

Wreckage

Storm clouds gone wrong, the giant faces rampaged across the sky—hungry, angry, and implacable. The inexplicable monsters appeared on the final lap of my morning run. Behind me, both Dawn and Alonso cursed, letting me know they saw it too. The bulbus faces lunged toward the Earth, jaws wide and sharp like snapping turtles' beaks in the distorted facial forms of men. Across the sky, I saw three distinct monstrous visages made up of air and water or perhaps some essence unknown to modern man—a culmination of wrath made physical.

"What... what are those?" Dawn's voice trembled, yet the pound of her sneakers on the street didn't slow.

"Cara?" Alonso grabbed my arm. "Are you seeing that?"

"Yes," I replied as I jerked to a stop. My ponytail swung against my sweaty shoulders, evoking the feeling of a hand patting my back. The sensation was no comfort. The monstrous evolutions in the sky were silent, not even a puff of wind to relieve the nothingness that condensed around us.

In all my life, I'd never seen something equal to the impossible cloud monsters. My fingers itched for my camera, from which I'd made my living in war zones and rainforests alike. Destruction was always easier to process from behind a lens.

Dawn ran two paces past me, staring at the sky. Her legs moved as though she had forgotten them. Beside me Alonso's breath rushed, loud as a scream in the silence. I didn't want him there, touching me, at the end of the world. He had begun jogging with us only a few months prior. It had started as an idle flirtation with me and grown into something much more dangerous, something that still wasn't breaking my wedding vows. Not yet.

I'd never mentioned my wife to him, but I wore my wedding ring plain to see. Ressia and I hadn't been happy in years. Our marriage was a cold war with both of us entrenched so deeply that escape wasn't an option. On occasion, I enjoyed the thrill of verbally testing the waters outside our plagued union—though I never dove in. I realized I never would have taken that plunge. Because it was Ressia who came to mind, the memory of her face and her heat against my back in bed, that stirred me from my stupor.

"Come on! We need shelter," I yelled to them, or whispered, and compelled my frozen legs into a run. My house was less than a block away.

One of the faces dipped, scraping over the land. Its jaws plowed through trees and sent up bits of homes as easily as a child would kick up sand at the beach. The rending, crunching sounds broke the unnatural silence. Then it lifted a house. The roof and walls cracked but went with the nightmare creature into the sky. Debris cascaded down—sad little teardrops of plaster and wood. Another face in the sky swept toward the ground.

I didn't watch their progress. Despite what I'd just seen, home meant safety. I had to make it there.

My peripheral vision showed the monsters continue plunging and ripping. I couldn't hear Dawn or Alonso behind me. In that moment, I didn't care if they were following. The sounds of destruction, snapping, booming, and crushing overlaid the frantic sounds of my heart and breath.

Our three bedroom "dream-home" had been meant to hold more than two bitter women. It was made for children—as Ressia often reminded me.

I reached my front door and flung it open.

Inside the air was stale and boozy. I crashed at Dawn's house the night before. The evidence of my absence lay across the coffee table: an empty wine bottle rocking drunkenly on its side, a half-empty fifth of gin next to one of our crystal wedding glasses, and pillows scattered over the leather sofa—the typical debris of our ongoing war. Ressia stood beyond the couch in front of the kitchen window. The pink ends of her blonde hair were matted. A mug dangled from her fingers and a small puddle of coffee—no doubt laced—pooled onto the hardwood.

Without turning she spoke, voice hysterical with laughter, "Should I be Chicken Little or should you? Because the sky is falling."

I wanted to dash over and take her in my arms. I could actually hear myself telling her that everything would be all right. The words never left my mouth because in that instant, Dawn darted in behind me followed by Alonso. The distance between my wife and me seemed too vast to cross, and the distance littered with wreckage. How did one bridge a sea of broken promises, words used as weapons, absences little bombs that had cracked and broken away at our foundation, and walls build up against mutual destruction? And this wreckage, like that outside, was laid out in plain view.

Instead of going to Ressia, my eyes found my camera. I lifted it from the side table. Deftly, without much thought, my hands switched the standard lens for a wide angle. I walked around the couch, the opposite end from Ressia and the kitchen, and approached the sliding door onto the patio.

"What the hell are those things?" Dawn asked. "My phone can't connect..."

With my camera in my hands, fear fell away. I was invulnerable. I opened the door and slipped out beneath the fragile covering of the patio roof. I began to take pictures of the hungry cloud faces as they ravaged the land.

"Is this happening elsewhere? Everywhere?" Dawn asked.

As if that mattered. The clouds were hungry giants here and now. And in such a moment, here and now is everywhere and eternal. Perhaps the others agreed, because no one answered her. Some moments were too big to permit contemplation of the future. They could swallow a person whole. Only my camera gave me the distance to process anything but the nearest face as it fell from the sky and then rose again with a mouthful of our world.

"Is there a basement?" Alonso asked.

How like a man to think he could solve the end of the world. In normal conditions, such a thought would have embarrassed me, but my tiny sexism hardly mattered under those snapping jaws.

"There's a wine cellar… so, yes," Dawn said. "We'd be safer. Ressia? Come on, honey."

"Cara?" Ressia said.

How like her to need me to approve of her actions. How like her to want more from me. But I had nothing to give. My camera captured several action shots of one face crashing its jaws around a water tower and the water spraying outward.

"Cara, are you coming?" Dawn asked. "It isn't safe."

The shutter of my camera whirred. A small cellar wouldn't save us if those monsters came our way. And what was the purpose of prolonging our existences by burrowing into fear? It would only trap us within this moment. How could I explain that there was something achingly beautiful in destruction? I knew the "sky was falling," but it only took a glance around my house to show I was used to looming destruction. When a situation was too big to change, too terrifying to address, a masochistic loveliness remained in watching all that was once lovely and safe be uprooted and slowly dismantled.

This beauty was only safe to view through a lens.

Without a word, I pointed my camera inside and captured Ressia's image. Her coffee cup still dangled from her fingers, swinging and ready to fall and shatter on the floor. Behind her was the polluted coffee table and the couch that she'd probably slept on, just as I'd slept on Dawn's. All this evidence of the harm we'd done to each other was there, but her face, oh her face—high cheekbones, full-lips and, sad brown eyes—her face seemed infinitely beautiful to me.

I replaced the lens cap on my camera and walked over to my wife. I took her hand and squeezed.

The sky had been falling for a long time.

Awake

Originally published in Once Upon Now

Rose

Garbled by a vast distance, a voice pierced the shroud over Rose's mind. The still darkness around her weighed down her limbs and froze her lips. Without the ability to speak or move, all Rose could do was listen.

She shoved aside the comforting nothing and strained to comprehend Crane's heated words. The anger in her husband's voice bit out into the dimness, burning off layers of haziness until the sound rang through her.

"I refuse to believe there's no solution," Crane said.

The rage of his tone smacked against Rose, but beneath it was something that hurt her more—a deep weariness. If her hands hadn't weighed a million tons, she would have lifted them to comfort him, smooth his wild curls.

"I'm sorry, Crane," another man said. His voice had the slight crackle that came with advanced age. "You have enough medical training to understand what these signs mean. You've read her vitals. I can't refute anything the doctors have told you. Refusing the truth won't help you or Rose."

Rose stretched out mentally, pressing against limbs as responsive as stone. Pounding against her eyelids—steel shutters to her lonely world. If only she could find a crack, a single weak point, and could move. She could rush to Crane, tell him death came for everyone in their turn, that she loved him and had never blamed him.

"I have done everything the medical doctors asked," Crane's voice was closer now. *"Everything.* I won't accept she's getting worse, that…"

"I think you need to prepare yourself for the inevitable. Her brain is shutting down. It's not what I want to say, but it's true. This must be very hard for you, but she's already weakening. From the readings, within a few weeks, even if she wakes up, she won't be your wife anymore."

The voices faded until they were a no more than a hum under the warm blanket of her mind.

Was she brain damaged? She didn't know how to test the idea. Crane was the smart one. He'd always said she was the heart, but she had silently disagreed. That was him too. And now all Rose could be was a weight around his neck, a grief that wouldn't fade because her stupid body insisted on remaining alive.

If stopping her lungs from drawing air were possible, she would have. Crane should be able to continue with his life. In spite of the despair cloaking her, she had memories to live on. Would Crane allow himself that comfort? He'd always blamed himself for her disappointments.

His voice, even without words, hummed in the background as days passed and brought back swelling memories of their life.

She recalled their honeymoon. He'd taken her five miles from town to a bed-and-breakfast for a long-weekend. It rained the whole trip—a freezing rain with a biting wind. They'd laid under a floral comforter together, and she'd told him about all the wonderful vacation spots in her travel magazines—places they'd go someday. It wasn't until she found Crane studying her vacation notebooks that she realized he had no idea how perfect that time was for her. He thought he'd failed her.

Sure, she liked to daydream of distant locales and five-star hotels that cost more than he made in a month, but a day in the rain with him beat any exotic location without him. Crane was her real dream. He was a warm, steady home filled with love and acceptance. If only she'd been able to make him see.

"Rose, it's not ready," Crane's voice filtered in.

She imagined his soft palm, the skin dry from too much hand-sanitizer.

"What else can I do?"

Tears burned inside her, unspent, clogging the emptiness with words that frothed behind the dam of her unresponsive lips.

"If I'd just come home an hour sooner that day, you would be fine. I cannot give up now... this was the point of it all—you. Always you, Rose. The machine isn't ready to be tested. The dispersal of energy is wrong; the fluctuations must be less extreme in the final distribution."

As Crane moved, something crashed, shattered. Unseen, glass shards flew all over the room. A room she'd never seen.

Crane had moved to this house in what had seemed like a bribe to Rose's spirit. She'd begged him for years to move to Able's Hollow. The university had a reputation for accommodating research scientists. He could teach and work on his projects. But he'd refused.

Rose smiled at the memory though her lips never twitched.

"Able's Hollow?" Crane had said, his foppish brown hair falling over his glasses as they walked through the woods surrounding their house. Ahead of them was a small wooden bridge.

"I've looked at the statistics," Rose had said. "Temperate weather—so not too cold for me in the winter or too hot for you in the summer. It's only an hour from your folks and less than two from mine—"

"No, Rose."

"Can you really be so superstitious?"

"My brother still calls me the family's Ichabod. Ichabod Crane, a teacher and intellectual—"

"I've read *the Legend of Sleepy Hollow*," she said. Though she hadn't. She had seen the movie. "A town's name is a stupid thing to inhibit us. The university here won't let you do anything. Six times this week you've mentioned you need a new position. We could be happy there."

"We are happy here." Crane stepped up onto the bridge, gazing across the stream where a patch of wild strawberries beckoned them.

"I'd be happier on the other side of the bridge." Rose dropped his hand and ran over the wooden boards.

Berries filled her memory. They had been the sweetest she ever tasted, often taken from his fingers or lips while the water gurgled at their trespass.

In the distance, over the streams admonishments, she heard Crane's machine turn on—a low whir and several clacks. Those noises didn't belong in the memory; they belonged to the cold black world after Rose's accident. The stream faded as did the ghost taste of berries. A clatter of metal on metal.

"I love you so much, Rose. This needle should do it. This will integrate the necessary compound into your system. My life for yours. It should be enough, but there are so many errors. I can't get the one-to-one ratio I need. And the variation… I'm not sure what will happen anymore, but we can't wait. The process takes six days. Six days never seemed so long. Just hold on…"

Consciousness dimmed, pulled from her. Time passed without her full comprehension. It might have been days or weeks. In the emptiness, a vacuum of time that spanned forever, something pricked her arm, shooting rivers of ice with jets of bubbling heat through her. The dark boiled, bubbled, and swallowed her.

A wave of light hit her, and her eyelids fluttered. Rose stirred inside herself. The dark stripped away, leaving her naked. The back of her heel slammed into a hard surface as she kicked out, and ripples traveled up her body, like a reverberation through gelatin. She lay on her back in a shallow tub, and above her the gray ceiling came into focus.

Rose sat up, her mouth hanging open, flapping as she struggled for air. A clash of color assailed her eyes. Red and green flashed, and all around her a gooey, blue liquid glowed. A few wires snaked through the blue, fixing themselves to her pale flesh.

Sounds like half-formed words fell from her—five years of

thoughts and desires clashing for release from lips that had not moved in just as long.

Her body shook, causing the gel to quiver. Light reflected from its surface, dazzling her eyes.

"Crane?" she croaked, her first sensible utterance.

Other than clinging bits of gel, she was naked and her arms crossed over her bare chest. She blinked and squinted, trying to make sense of the jumble of machinery around her. Metal panels dotted with lights, displays, and buttons lined three of the room's four walls and linked to a central panel on her left. She shoved herself up out of the bath and forced her legs to hold her.

Just on the other side of the control panel, Crane lay in a similar construct to hers, only his was empty of the blue gel and no wires were affixed to him.

Rose stumbled out of the tub over to him and grabbed his hand. No response. What had he said about the machine?

She slapped her forehead, but the jarring brought no more insight into the machine. He'd told her about most of it, in terms only other scientists would understand. All she knew was that the gel conducted energy without having to convert the form of the energy.

"Crane," she repeated with more force. She shook his shoulders, and his head lolled lazily to the side.

Not so much as a facial twitch. She leaned into the tub, pressing her torso to him and her lips against his. He had to wake up. She wouldn't let him sacrifice himself. The subtle rise and fall of his chest told her he wasn't dead, but she knew all too well that a coma wasn't really life. She had to undo it. Only he'd never said anything about rectifying the project if it went awry. Was this what he'd intended?

Tears trickled down Rose's cheeks. She kissed him again, tasting the salt of her own tears on his lips but no other change.

"My life isn't worth yours. It never was. Please, how do I undo this?"

She sobbed until her throat was raw and the cold of the lab had numbed her bare flesh. She walked to a table near the doorway. A sundress, covered in flowers, a pair of white sandals, a cardigan and her makeup bag had been arranged across the surface. She dressed, not touching the bag. In fact, a flush crept up her cheeks on seeing it there.

Every day, Crane had done her makeup for her. She knew this not because she had felt his touch but because, on occasion, he'd talked about it. Like the time her favorite lipstick color was discontinued, and he'd sounded on the verge of crying telling her.

A series of lights over the lab door lit as she approached. When the final one went green the sealed lab door opened soundlessly to reveal a basement room, containing a few pieces of artwork from their previous home and a washer-dryer unit. In the doorway her head spun, and a heavy weariness descended. Her body informed her that though she had been sleeping for what must have been years, it was exhausted. A few wobbly steps toward the stairs left her barely able to stand.

This was no place to collapse. Not with Crane in the other room. So she turned, gathered her strength and stumbled to the doorway. A burst of energy hit her at the threshold, and she paused, gripping the door frame.

Maybe she could make it to Crane. That way if he woke, he would not be alone. But as she entered the room, her strength returned. With growing horror, she stared at the blue goo and the dangling cords. The shots he'd given her must keep her connected to the machine. Even without the bath and wires, she was still feeding off Crane.

"I can't leave this room." The door slid automatically shut behind her as she stumbled into the room.

Instead of going to Crane, Rose moved over to the machine. There was a large flashing display with rhythmically altering numbers. A timer. Rose closed her eyes and pressed her fingers to the side of her head.

Had Crane said something about this? He couldn't have intended her to remain in here forever, so it stood to reason the process wasn't complete. Could the numbers indicate the time left until her changes finalized? Rose sighed, despite escaping the heavy fatigue she'd experienced outside the lab, she was still tired. Answers were more likely to come after a proper rest.

She returned to Crane and knelt on the linoleum floor. With her head rested on his chest she drifted off into a light fitful sleep. Dreams haunted her, featuring scattered memories—twisted and torn. Memories of working the beauty pageant circuit, the cold judging stares, her mother's vocal disappointment when she lost mixed with ones of Crane's fingers massaging her shoulders as she curled against him to watch TV.

A crash from upstairs startled Rose from the whirling dreams, so unlike the emptiness of her coma. Rose trembled and clutched at Crane's hand. What sounded like hundreds of men trouped above her head. The thudding footfalls hit, and in the stillness resounded like the steps of giants.

After shaking the remaining veil of sleep from her mind, Rose forced her exhausted muscles over to the light switch and flipped it off, leaving her in a darkness that flickered with neon flashes from the machine. A low wattage row of lights turned on, painting a pathway through the chamber.

"Is this place hidden?" She dashed down the pathway until she came even with Crane. She struggled to remember what the lab door had looked like from the outside. She was reasonably sure the door was camouflaged on the basement side, but still her stomach clenched with nerves.

Muffled voices filtered through the walls. Why were people in the house? It didn't make sense.

In the faint light, Rose caught her reflection on the mirrored surface of the control panel. The face there ripped a gasp from her throat. She hadn't expected the healthy, youthful face of her beauty queen days. But the skinny wraith she saw shocked her —how could she have lost so much weight? She'd never been so dreadfully thin. Mascara dotingly applied by Crane ran in streaks over her face, and a slight lip stain was the only color on her ghostly flesh. Her cheeks were hollow and high enough to make a model proud. At thirty, when her accident put her in a coma, she'd been happily putting on weight—an extra fifteen pounds meant she could eat like everyone else, and Crane and she both got fewer insulting comments about trophy wives or Beauty and the Beast. Now, that fifteen pounds and more had fled.

Rose bit her knuckles and looked away. The crashing upstairs continued, but after a while noises like a rough search came from outside the lab door. Someone was banging around the washer and dryer doors.

A sob rioted inside her throat. Whoever those people were, they didn't sound friendly. If Crane had enemies, he'd never mentioned it, but she couldn't risk it. Not with him in this condition.

Another person pounded down the unseen stairs to the basement. Briefly all went quiet.

Rose shoved her fist further between her teeth.

"Anything down here?" barked a loud, crisp male voice. Each word like a hammer blow to Rose.

A reply blocked by the wall came but was unintelligible.

Rose closed her eyes.

One after the other, people hammered up the stairs. For a little while longer they swept the house, but soon it was silent.

Rose wept. Alone in a tomb, she waited.

A few hours passed before footsteps sounded above. No crashes this time, just slow, methodical taps.

"What's happening, Crane? What do I do?" Rose's hands twisted in Crane's shirt but no matter how hard she searched he gave no visible response.

Someone came down, slower than the previous group. Rose stood, her legs gummy but functional. Perhaps the person was not a friend, but what other choice remained? Sit in the lab until Crane died of dehydration? No. She had to do something.

"I can't be alone in here. I need help," she explained to her sleeping husband.

She moved to the door, clicked the Daryl and let it slide open.

∞∞∞

Alex

Alex Valera came to Able's Hollow in the quiet stasis before dawn. Like the world itself slept. The timing fit the assignment, and he smiled at the dim glow on the horizon, wishing his old FBI partner and current wife, Gina, was there to be annoyed at his shenanigans.

Wrappers from the gas station burritos sat in the passenger seat. He'd rolled down the window but the steady howl didn't give him the distraction of human interaction. As soon as he arrived in Able's Hollow, he'd send Gina an inane text—it would relieve the worry swirling inside him.

He'd played around with calling the town Sleepy Hollow. In fact, he'd called Gina at home to tell her his next assignment was in 'Sleepy Hollow.' Baby Anna had been crying in the background, and it should have cued him that Gina was in no mood.

"Don't be ridiculous," she'd snapped.

"Headless horsemen would be too fantastical even for me, Gina. But there are a heck of a lot of sleeping people." He smiled as the word 'heck' came naturally from his mouth. Eleven months with a child had gutted his vocabulary and set him up with a whole new set of 'swell' words.

"Sleepy Hollow was the name of the town, not the people's condition." Gina sighed. "Get some good food in you on the drive, you hear?"

He had been smart enough not to ask her to define *good*. But as he pulled into Able's Hollow in the eerie light, he wished there was something other than burritos and coffee in his stomach. His gut flip-flopped as he reached the edge of town and a roadblock. He flashed his FBI contractor's credentials at the roadblock. The queasy lurching intensified as he drove onto the empty streets.

The first curved outline etched on the sidewalk might have been mistaken for hopscotch squares from a distance. It wasn't. The markings didn't denote a child's game but the outline of a human form. More white body tracings dotted the road as he drove. They covered everything.

He pulled up to the hospital—a small affair, lit like a lone star. Even from the edge of the parking lot, filled with abandoned cars. He saw the bodies on stretchers, spilling from the hospital's halls.

This assignment was going to get nasty. A lot of lives were on the line.

Hopefully, the Marines could airlift the residents out today —this town was incapable of giving life support to so many. He'd know more soon, and if he had any luck, before the CDC arrived to jam up the works. The future of over five thousand people depended on a timely solution—something the government consistently bumbled.

A whole town *didn't* just fall asleep. No outward evidence of injury or drug. Not a single case in the surrounding towns which made a normal illness unlikely.

Daryl Downy met him in the parking lot. Daryl had been Alex's contact within the FBI since Gina used her pregnancy to bow out of their working partnership.

"Even for you this case is weird." Daryl opened Alex's car door. No greeting.

"I can't judge yet how weird. Give me what you know so far." Alex followed Daryl across the parking lot to Daryl's car.

"The citizens are stable. But many, especially the younger ones, aren't doing well. Whatever happened seemed not to affect infants, so we've divided them off, but we don't have enough staff to care for them. A few neighborhoods at the outskirts of town weren't affected. The rest of the citizens are effectively asleep, not even as deep as a coma, and yet they are unwakable. We've found the point of origin. We investigated and—"

"If your next words include a sleeping princess and a loom, I'm bailing." Alex grinned extra wide to compensate from the glower on Daryl's face.

"No 'princess'. What we found was an empty home. From the house there is a two-mile radius that encompasses the affected areas. The neighborhoods that weren't touched were outside the radius. We had a few houses sitting on the line in which some family members were affected while others were not."

"Let's get over to that house."

As soon as Alex buckled himself in, he took in a deep breath and tried to avoid looking back into the hospital. The stakes were clear, better to focus. Emotions were always better saved for after a job.

"The owners of the house," Alex started, "what's the scoop on them?"

"Married couple. No children. The husband is a scientist employed at the local college. Hasn't been doing any research projects for the school though, just teaching. Years back, he did work with lab animals a while back, transferring energy from a meal eaten by one group being transferred to make a second group feel satiated. The transfer rates didn't please him though since almost 90% of the energy was lost in the transfer over. Plus, when the transfer device powered down often the results would revert, leaving the original group with all the energy and the transfer group with no long-term benefit. No experiments on file after that one."

"And his better half?"

"High school beauty queen. She married at twenty and co-owned a jewelry store. Five years ago, a tree limb fell on her. She's been in a coma ever since. Her husband signed her into home care. The most recent doctor's report said her condition was deteriorating. She was alive when this," he motioned with his arm to the town, "happened."

"Right-o. Thanks,"

"Don't thank me, Mr. Valera. If it were up to me, you wouldn't be here. Official story is chemical spill. I'd rather just go with that and let the CDC handle the victims."

"So, what are the names of this husband and wife?" Alex asked, ignoring the insult.

Daryl pulled up to a split-level home. The windows and drapes were closed tight. The lawn had gone to seed, and patches were yellowed grass packed against the soil. It might as well be spray-painted with 'Go Away' on its siding.

"Professor Crane Brier and Rose Brier."

Alex choked on a laugh. Seriously? His brain couldn't settle between the sleeping beauty comparison and that of Sleepy Hollow. Crane? Briar? "Briar?"

"B-R-I-E-R."

Didn't matter.

He climbed out of the car and ambled up the overgrown path to the doorway. He glanced at the edges of the yard, half-hopeful he'd find a pumpkin patch. Though there was no one to tell the Sleepy Hollow joke to anyhow. Being able to might have lifted the depression that was settling in around him.

Most of the time he worked better alone, but there were moments he missed having Gina at his side at work. He still remembered the day they'd assigned her, and he got his first look—pretty face, red hair pulled into an 'I don't take any shit' ponytail. The Mulder and Scully references amused him but grated on Gina as unprofessional. The moment she got pregnant, she'd finagled it into a way to go back to dull office work.

He hadn't minded. Their baby was adorable.

On the doorstop, he texted a quick message to his wife. *'No headless horsemen but there's a Professor Crane'* as he opened the front door and stepped inside. The light of her reply text illuminated a table coated with pictures—set-up like a shrine. A few had been knocked over, and one had broken, scattering glass over the floor.

'A girl named Aurora too?'

She was in a better mood, but looking at the photos, Alex didn't want to joke. His heart wasn't in the next text.

'No. But Crane's last name is Brier, pronounced briar.' Then as a separate text for impact, *'Her name's Rose.'*

'... Do your job.'

He tucked his phone away and flipped the lights to better see the rows of pictures. Every one of them depicted the same woman—must be Rose. Wedding snapshots from a courthouse affair sat next to professional stills of the toothy beauty. Over-made-up and too chipper, she stared out with vacant eyes, not surprising for a pageant head shot. He should have told Gina the 'beauty queen' part.

But the more recent photos were charming, the same bright grin, a little less makeup but real glitter in her eyes.

He lifted the picture with the broken glass from the floor, and a frown creased his face. Rose lay in a hospital bed—for once, not smiling. Her blonde hair hung limp around her wan face, and yet she retained a haunting beauty.

Alex set the image down with shaky hands, imagining Gina's face like that. Life passed so quickly and once it was gone, no one could get it back.

The idiot outside had said there was nothing here. There was. Crane and Rose were a recipe for mad science.

Alex wandered through the house, glancing in each room and jotting down his observations. Sparse furnishings dotted the space, and everything had a light covering of dust, but no mess except what Daryl and his buddies broke. No one lived in these rooms. No TV in the house, and the computer in the den looked neat and orderly.

One of the bedrooms had a smattering of medical equipment, but not the amount Alex would expect from a guy who kept a shrine to his wife. Something was off here. While possible, Crane could have kept Rose in that room, Alex doubted it. The carpet to and from the room wasn't worn and all the machines looked brand new—not a dent or a chip in sight. After five years, there should have been wear and tear.

Last was the basement—a worn path in the carpet led to the stairs. In the entire house, it was the only high traffic area. Alex descended after flipping on the light.

The basement walls were dingy, and a washer-dryer unit sat at the foot of the stairs—like a beacon of white in the room, also from tiny chinks in the paint and a small dent. Alex guessed this was the only appliance in the house that got regular use. A garbage can filled with takeout boxes was wedged between laundry baskets. The right wall was made of stone, and cracks riddled the mortar. However, the tapestry on the left wall captured his attention.

He gave a light whistle. Not a cheap piece; the ode to sleeping beauty might be handed down from generations, a wealthy man's gift, or an insight into Prof. Brier's mind. Sure it was a depiction of the familiar story, but not focused on the princess waking. The beautiful maiden was absent. No, the focal point was the briar hedge, the wall that barred anyone from reaching the maiden.

The professor had been trying to wake his wife. Alex had no doubts on that front. One 'sleeping' woman who couldn't wake married to a brilliant scientist and with them being at the center of a town of newly comatose people could be added up to different things. Yet, Crane's last experiment had been transferring energy from one group to another. Once his wife fell into a coma, why wouldn't he focus in on trying to fix her? Alex knew in his gut this was all about waking Rose. Which meant finding Prof. Brier was essential.

The secret had to be somewhere here. Clearly not in sight or the FBI would have found it in their run-through. If Crane hadn't been keeping Rose in a Hospital or the room upstairs, where was he keeping her? All signs pointed to this basement being the only place he frequented. Maybe a room, tucked away. The wise thing was to get the house plans to find missing square footage.

Doing that entailed pulling Daryl back in, and Alex wanted to handle the professor alone.

The time it would take for the government to move on anything might be too long for some victims. What about the young ones that Daryl had said weren't doing well? Or the babies that no one was available to tend to?

This was a delicate business, and with so many lives involved, the FBI would never see Professor Crane as anything but a villain. Someone to be stopped. But maybe he was the only one who could stop what was happening in time. Which left Alex playing lone hero trying to find the mystical 'wizard.'

"Well," he said to himself, "ask my wife any day, I'm no prince. How do I get past the briar wall?"

"For starters, that's the wrong wall."

The soft female voice emitted from behind him, which was a blessing as the speaker didn't see Alex pale and grab at his chest or his hand slide down to the gun holstered over his hip. By the time he turned, his breathing was even.

The woman wore a flowered shift dress, which hung on her like a bag. She leaned on the doorframe—a door that hadn't existed moments before. Despite the wall's support, she swayed from the effort of standing. Her skinny legs trembled. Even with the weight loss, and pale pallor. Rose Brier. Her blonde hair toppled in tangles over her shoulders, and her makeup looked as if it had seen her through a hard night of partying.

"Well," he said, "Check you out. It's not every day I meet Sleeping Beauty."

Rose sighed at the joke, knuckles going white as she clung to the doorframe. "And you are? Given you've broken into my home, the least you can do is introduce yourself."

"Alex, ma'am. I've been called in to investigate last night's incident."

"You're a detective?"

"Something like. I contract with the government and take jobs they can't or won't handle."

She froze, studying his face until he wiped the corners of his mouth to make sure no trace of burrito lingered there.

"Come inside. You'll want to see Crane's machine."

"Not a spindle, is it?" Alex said. Gina would have kicked him in the shin.

Rose glared and turned into the lab. By the time Alex reached the doorway, halogen glow lit the room.

A giant mechanical contraption filled his vision. Dozens of displays flashed on the wall. Two tables took central position with a glowing podium between them. A man's body lay on one of them. Alex approached and looked in at a thin man. Asleep. And probably the professor. "Shit."

He peered at the other table and reached out to touch the inch thick layer of blue goo. Cords trailed out of it. From the state of Rose's hair, she'd been in there, linked up. But why then wasn't Prof. Brier linked as well?

Alex checked carefully over Prof. Brier and the surrounding space. There were wires present, that appeared to be intended for him, yet they hung down, brushing the ground.

"What've you and your husband been tampering with down here?"

"Not me. Why are you here?" Her hands balled at her sides. Her lips drew back, revealing perfect white teeth. "Do you know something about this machine?"

"You never came out of your coma, did you?" Alex asked. Not naturally, at least.

"No. Alex, was it? What are you doing here? I don't appreciate my questions being ignored."

Princesses did like manners. Alex resisted saying so.

"I'm here because last night every citizen in Able's Hollow fell into a coma. And lo-and-behold, I find you with this sci-fi machine and a goo filled bathtub... and you're awake."

Rose stared at him, eyes wide, then bit down on her lip. A muffled sound escaped her as she moved between him and Crane. "No, no, no. How could it have affected anyone not in this room?"

"CDC will be here in the morning to determine if it's contagious before air-lifting everyone out."

Rose's fingers folded around her husband's. She trembled, and Alex wanted to tell her that everything would be okay, but his gut told him that was a lie. This wasn't a fairy tale, and no happy ending awaited her.

"He never thought... It was just supposed to be him and me involved in this experiment." Rose drew in a deep, ragged breath. She looked to the side at a timer, just a flick of the eyes then she turned away.

"It isn't just the two of you."

"But the rest will wake up."

"How do you know that?" Alex pondered the timer but

couldn't get past the sinking feeling that with each number that ticked away he had less time. And there wasn't much time left. Certainly not enough to second guess himself. Less than half an hour remained.

"I... because it couldn't take a whole town to wake one person. My husband planned for this to be a one-to-one ratio—me and him. Crane assumed he wouldn't wake up. He told me so... but now maybe he will, since there were so many. Maybe all of them will wake up."

"You don't know that. Is your life worth nearly five thousand other lives?" An even worse ratio than the experiment Daryl had talked about. Something had gone horribly wrong here.

"I could see Crane again... I just want to see my husband."

"We must turn the machine off before that timer stops. I can't risk all those lives."

"Turning it off could be more dangerous than just letting it time out. What if it kills them?" Rose clung to her husband.

"Not if this is like his previous experiment on energy transfer. There are a lot of 'what ifs' right now. We don't have time for them. Are you going to help me?" Alex set his hand on his holstered gun. Using it on Rose... well that was something to avoid. Yet, he spoke truthfully. Even a princess wasn't worth sacrificing a whole town.

"You going to help me?" Alex asked. So far, she'd offered no resistance.

"I can figure what happens after that machine turns off. Either everyone dies and I go back into a coma or they wake up and I go back into a coma. After that, all the government types come to study Crane's invention. If we're lucky and Crane wakes up, he'll spend the rest of his life in some sort of government detention." Her back was to him and her long hair hung down over her shoulders onto her husband and the lab table.

"This isn't a choice." Alex drew the gun but left it lowered. She didn't need to see it yet. "There's nothing wrong with those people out there, so they should wake up. But if we leave it on, we risk you taking too much, and they'll all stay comatose."

"So you want me to sacrifice myself, not even knowing for sure if it will help anyone?"

"It sounds ugly, but yes. That's what I'm asking. I'm sorry."

"Do me one favor?"

"If I can," Alex averted his eyes. What if it was Gina? He couldn't refuse her anything reasonable. Not this woman, who another man had been willing to sacrifice everything for. He had to honor the value of something beloved. "This goes above my paygrade soon."

"Tell Crane it worked—before you do whatever you do with him. And that I regained consciousness. Tell him no one forced me… and tell him I heard him all those years. I know how hard he tried to get me back—how much he loved me."

"I'll give him the message."

"He talked about this project, all the things I could do when it was complete. All the places I could go… as if I'd want to travel anywhere without him."

"Back on point, as sorry as I am for you, thousands of people might die if we don't solve this. Do you know how to turn this thing off?"

"You should be able to power it down from the control panel here."

Rose climbed onto the table where Crane lay, and Alex wished Gina was next to him. In that moment, he needed to hold her, to be sure she was still there. Rose snuggled in close beside Crane, positioning his arm around her. Did Alex have the strength to do what Rose was doing? To walk calmly into something that meant losing himself? A desire to apologize to Crane bubbled inside him.

This sleeping beauty walked to her spindle with full knowledge. She'd never get her prince charming. If only Gina had been there to tease him for getting sentimental, but she wasn't, and he swore that when he got home, he'd make sure he didn't miss any of those precious moments. Moments Rose and Crane would have died for. Alex would find a way to be home more, to see Anna's first steps.

For the first time, he understood why Gina had wanted that office job. Living, real living was coming home to the ones you loved every day—being with them. His work, that wasn't life, it was his version of a coma and he wanted to be awake.

∞∞∞

Rose

Crane's arm fell over her, loose and unresponsive, but she could pretend he was holding her. If he'd been able to, she knew he would have. As it was, it would have to be enough having his warm breath against her neck. She would save that sensation in her mind.

"If this works..." Alex said.

"If this works, I'll be back where I was before. I'll die without ever waking up again." Rose pulled Crane's arm tighter around her, but even so, the trembling of her voice signaled the mounting fear that commanded her to run, run far, far away. "Crane used to talk about relative worth—how the worth of any object depends on the viewer. I know what I was worth to him... But I can't believe he would have sacrificed a whole town for me. I certainly won't make that sacrifice. To my view, I wouldn't be worth much if I was willing to risk all those lives."

Alex nodded. His eyes glistened, and he wiped at them. "I've never killed someone."

"I'm sorry."

"Me too." Alex moved up to the control panel.

"85262 is the passcode to get you in." Rose snuggled Crane but found the position unsatisfying. If she could never see him again, she wanted to gaze into his face now. Memorize every line and keep it with her until her mind went blank. She turned over on her other side and tucked her face against Crane's neck.

The panel beeped with each number Alex pressed.

"You ready?" Alex asked.

"Yes."

Rose snuggled closer against Crane and wrapped her arms around him.

"Nothing happened. It won't take the passcode," Alex said. "What else could it be?"

"The numbers that correspond to Rose B, maybe?"

The keypad let off little beeps again, and once more nothing happened. Rose struggled for another guess at a passcode. Her eyes flicked to the timer. Not much time left now, less than a minute.

"Screw this, cover your ears, Princess," Alex said.

Rose opened her mouth to ask why when she saw the gun lift. Was he going to shoot the console? Would that work? If the console powered down, would it start the shutdown sequence for the machine? No time to ask.

She covered her ears.

A shower of sparks erupted, accompanied by a resounding boom that echoed in the metal room, and Rose's eyes squeezed closed. Her ears rang. But even without her hearing, she could feel the vibration. The rhythmic tick of a countdown commenced.

Beep.

"I love you," she whispered.

Beep.

Rose bit her lip.

Beep.

"Please go on, whatever happens. Live your life."

Beep.

She brushed her lips over his—one last moment of warmth to take with her. The sound of the machine faded. With the outer hum dimming, a familiar inner fog swelled to greet her. Darkness swarmed over her, but for just an instant, she could still feel Crane's warm against her skin. Feel his arm tighten around her. His mouth pressed to hers.

She knew what the passcode was. AWAKE. It came to her as the deep sleep overcame her.

Rose fell back into the nothingness.

Join Jesse's Mailing List

Want more?

That's not problem! There is plenty more insanity to be had.

Sign up for Jesse's mailing list (or reader's group as she likes to call it) for updates on her latest projects and extra perks like character interviews, early release information, insights into her process, and best yet FREE exclusive short stories!

Did you miss reading her other works? Click here for Beneath 5th City

Books By This Author

Beneath 5Th City

Spider's Kiss

Spider's Gambit

Spider's Choice

Blind Black

Monsters Movies & Mayhem

Once Upon Now

The Best Gift...

Is a review.

Enjoyed the book? Please remember that reviews are the lifeblood of any indie author as they are how readers find new books and decide what is right for them. So say what you likes, what you didn't like, or anything else you feel might be helpful. Even leaving a star rating can help!

Printed in Great Britain
by Amazon